Supposing...

From the author of *Ounce Dice Trice* (a book of unusual and magical words) comes *Supposing...* (a book of speculation, mischief, and paradox). Legendary illustrator and designer Bob Gill's drawings give life to Alastair Reid's mind-opening musings and wonders. Together Reid and Gill make *Supposing...* a delightful introduction to the manifold pleasures of the unfettered imagination.

Praise for *Ounce Dice Trice*

"I want every children's book editor and also every primary and middle school teacher and librarian in America to read this book. It is the antidote to plodding, plot-driven, two-line synopsizable, anti-imagination books. *Ounce Dice Trice* can be read cover to cover, back to front, middle to end, upside down, any way you like."   – Daniel Pinkwater, NPR

"*Ounce Dice Trice* was designed to amuse and the words belong on the borderline where 'the poet and the child meet.'"   – The New York Times

"The book is like an explosion of language, but with a sense of order behind it."   – Catherine Bohne, Community Bookstore, Brooklyn

This is a NEW YORK REVIEW BOOK
published by THE NEW YORK REVIEW OF BOOKS
435 Hudson Street, New York, NY 10014
www.nyrb.com

Library of Congress Cataloging-in-Publication Data

Reid, Alastair, 1926–
    Supposing / by Alastair Reid; illustrated by Bob Gill
        p. cm.—(New York Review Children's Collection)
    Summary: A child imagines many silly, impossible, and
even naughty things and their possible consequences,
from learning unusual languages to building a tiny boat
and sailing around the world.
    ISBN 978-1-59017-369-5 (alk. paper)
[1. Imagination—Fiction.] I.Gill, Bob, 1931– II. Title
PZ7.R2645Su 2010
[E]—dc22

ISBN 978-1-59017-369-5

Printed in the United States of America on acid-free paper
1 2 3 4 5 6 7 8 9 10

Supposing

I built my own rocket and went to the moon but didn't like it much and came home without telling anyone and just smiled to myself when other people talked about it...

Supposing

I built a small boat and sailed around the world and when I was a mile from the shore of my home town, and everybody was waiting for me with medals and cameras, I just turned the boat and sailed round again the other way…

Supposing

I went begging instead of going to school and drew pictures and sang songs on a street corner and people gave me money and one day my father came home and said he was ruined and I told him not to worry and led him to my room and showed him my trunk full of pennies and he laughed and laughed…

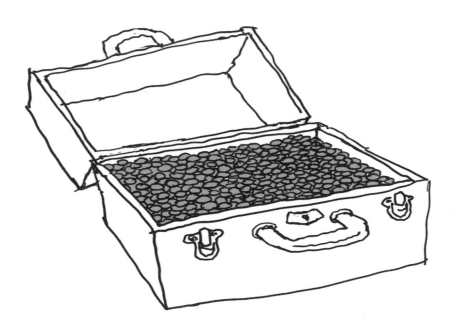

Supposing...

by Alastair Reid
Illustrated by Bob Gill

The New York Review Children's Collection
New York

Supposing

I collected old hair from a barber shop and sent it in parcels to people I didn't like...

Supposing

I could be any size I wanted to be…

Supposing

I looked in the mirror one day and saw someone who wasn't me at all and I said, *Who are you?* and he said, *Mr. Endicott...*

Supposing

I became a wise old professor who learned ancient languages and when some men digging up ruins found a big stone with funny writing on it that nobody understood they sent it to me to see what it said and I found it was a secret spell that explained how to vanish and when they pestered me to tell I just waved to them and vanished...

Supposing

I had a great house with valuable paintings
and furniture and things and I came
home one day and it was all blazing
and burned down and people came
rushing up to me being sorry for me
but I just laughed and took off my
clothes and threw them into the fire…

Supposing
I taught my dog how to read...

Supposing I got to be three hundred years old…

Supposing

I painted a picture of the view from my window and painted the river orange just for fun, and when I went out the next morning the river had really turned orange…

Supposing I went bald…

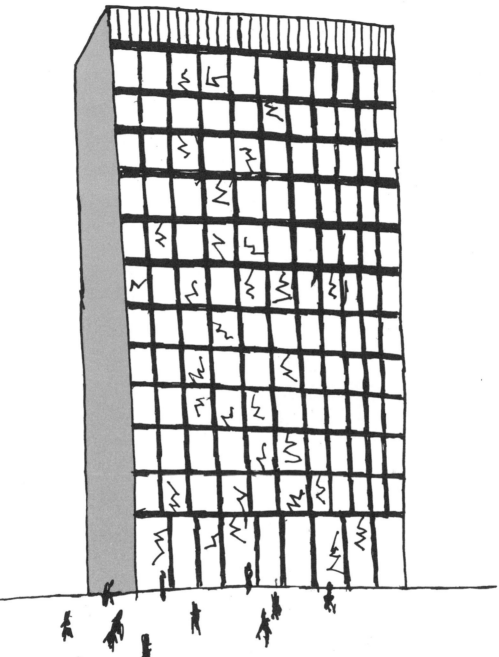

Supposing

I could make one special noise so shrill
that it broke glass and I never told
anybody and one day I went over to a
new glass skyscraper and made my noise…

Supposing
I had fur instead of skin...

Supposing
a very beautiful lady fell in love with me and wanted me to marry her but I just yawned and said maybe…

Supposing

I lived close to a circus and took scraps
every day to my favorite lion and learned
to speak Lion, and one night the lion
escaped and frightened people and I
ran up to the lion by myself and spoke
to it in Lion until it went to sleep and
the manager gave me a free ticket to
the circus for the rest of my life...

Supposing

I painted a picture of myself painting
a picture of myself painting a picture of
myself painting a picture of myself…

Supposing

a funny old fortune-teller told me I was going on a journey and just to bamboozle her I stayed home for the rest of my life…

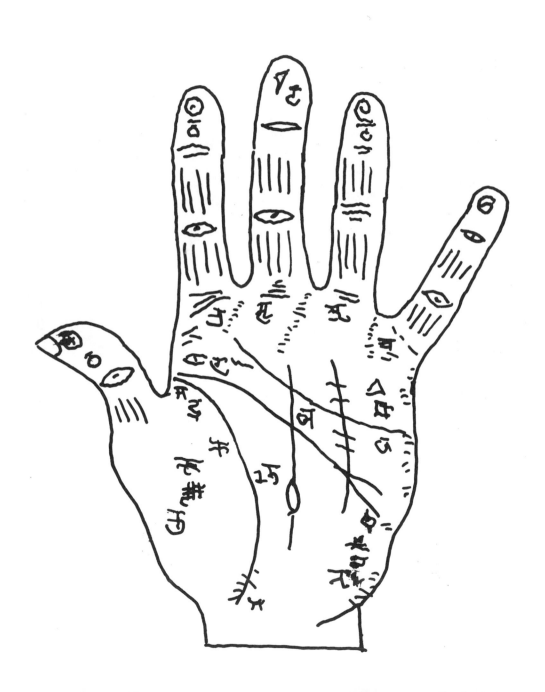

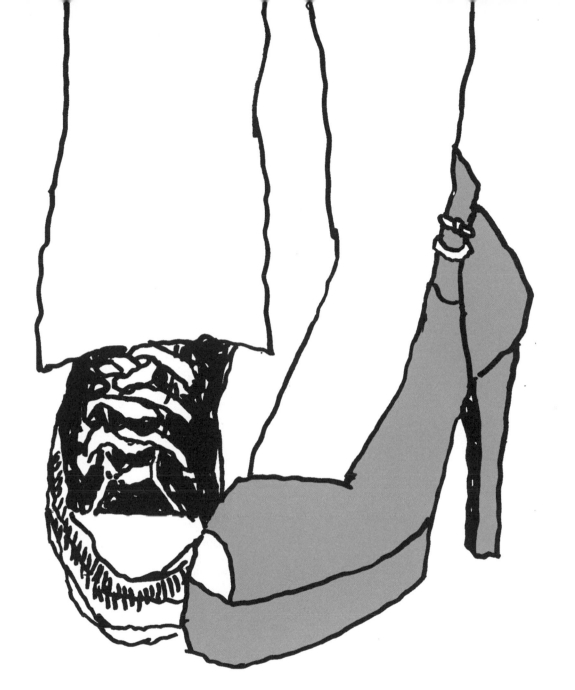

Supposing

I said something I shouldn't have at dinner,
and my mother kicked me under the table as she
sometimes does, and I said in a loud voice,
Mother, why are you kicking me under the table?...

Supposing

I became a famous scientist and knew all about the stars and looked through my telescope and saw that the world was going to end next Sunday, and told everybody but they all made fun of me, so when Sunday came I had a big dinner with all my favorite food and then sat at my telescope and just as I said the world ended...

Supposing

I were a millionaire and went to
a bank wearing old clothes and a
doorman was rude and wouldn't
let me in and I called the manager
on the phone and bought the bank
and went back in my old clothes
and when the doorman shouted
at me again, I said, very quietly,
You're fired…

Supposing

I could meet some of my ancestors…

Supposing

I hid a few of my treasures in a very secret place nobody could ever find, so secret that I can't find it myself…

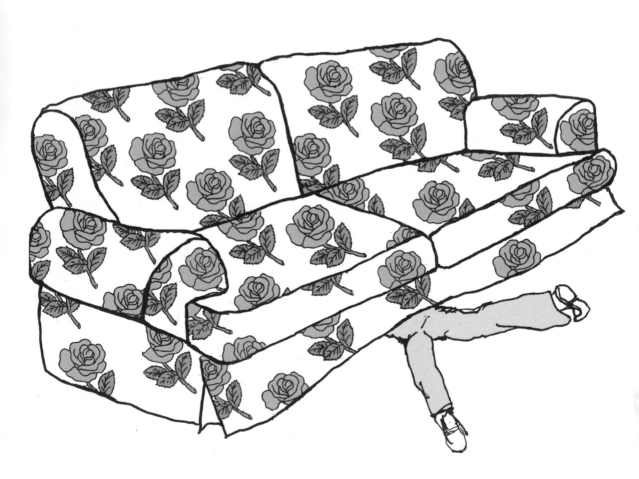

Supposing
I telephoned people I didn't know in the middle of the night and practiced my horrible sounds over the phone…

Supposing

I told a fussy woman on the train that I was an orphan and had no home and when I got off the train and went over to where our house was, there was nothing but trees and nobody had ever heard of me…

Supposing

I appeared on television answering questions and there was one question which nobody could answer and although I knew the answer instead of saying it I just burped...

Supposing

my Aunt Mabel came to tea and said to me
how big I was getting, for the millionth time,
and I just stared back and said to her, *How
old you're getting…*

Supposing

I had a twin brother but we never told anyone and only went to school half the time each…

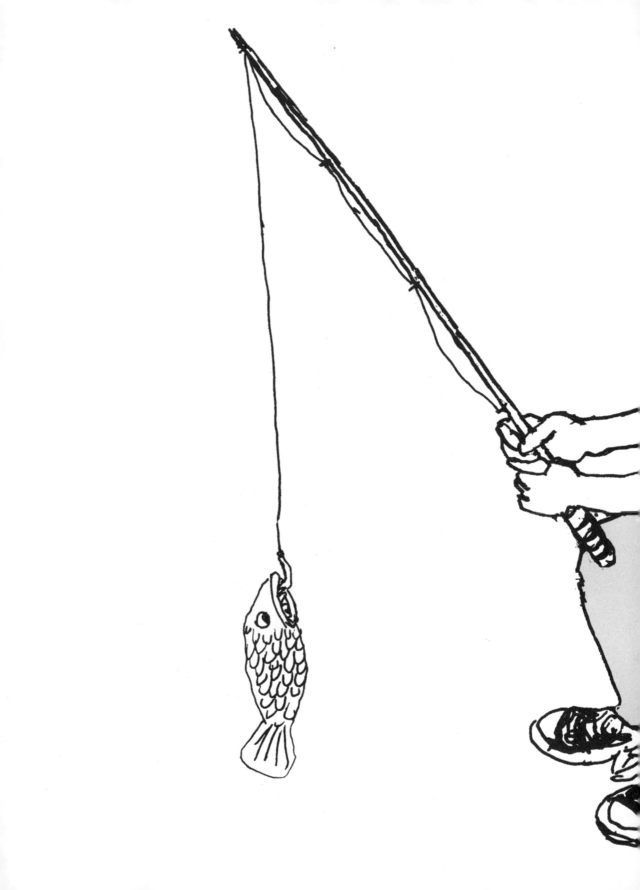

Supposing

I read a book about how to change into animals
and said a spell and changed myself into a cat
and when I climbed on the book to change myself
back I found I couldn't read...

Alastair Reid is a poet, a prose chronicler, a translator, and a traveler. Born in Scotland, he came to the United States in the early 1950s, began publishing his poems in *The New Yorker* in 1951, and for the next fifty-odd years was a traveling correspondent for that magazine. Having lived in both Spain and Latin America for long spells, he has been a constant translator of poetry from the Spanish language, in particular the work of Jorge Luis Borges and Pablo Neruda. He has published more than forty books, among them a wordbook for children, *Ounce Dice Trice,* with drawings by Ben Shahn. Most recently, in 2008, he published in the U.K. two career-spanning volumes, *Outside In: Selected Prose* and *Inside Out: Selected Poetry and Translations.* The substance of *Supposing . . .* he gleaned from the many children who have influenced him, to all of whom he owes and dedicates the text.

Bob Gill is a designer, illustrator, writer, filmmaker, teacher, and New Yorker. Of the many books he's written for designers, his favorite is *Forget all the rules you ever learned about graphic design, including the ones in this book.*

Titles in The New York Review Children's Collection

Esther Averill
Captains of the City Streets
The Hotel Cat
Jenny and the Cat Club
Jenny Goes to Sea
Jenny's Birthday Book
Jenny's Moonlight Adventure
The School for Cats

James Cloyd Bowman
*Pecos Bill: The Greatest
Cowboy of All Time*

Sheila Burnford
Bel Ria: Dog of War

Dino Buzzati
*The Bears' Famous Invasion
of Sicily*

**Ingri and
Edgar Parin d'Aulaire**
D'Aulaires' Book of Animals
D'Aulaires' Book of Norse Myths
D'Aulaires' Book of Trolls
Foxie: The Singing Dog
The Terrible Troll-Bird
Too Big
The Two Cars

Eilís Dillon
The Island of Horses
The Lost Island

Eleanor Farjeon
The Little Bookroom

Penelope Farmer
Charlotte Sometimes

Rumer Godden
An Episode of Sparrows
The Mousewife

Lucretia P. Hale
The Peterkin Papers

**Russell and
Lillian Hoban**
The Sorely Trying Day

**Ruth Krauss
and Marc Simont**
The Backward Day

**Munro Leaf and
Robert Lawson**
Wee Gillis

**Rhoda Levine
and Edward Gorey**
Three Ladies Beside the Sea